the FUNNY DRAWING BOOK

by JERRY WARSHAW

...WITH A LOT OF HELP FROM JOYCE AND ELIZABETH WARSHAW
...AND PHOTOS BY DICK MASEK.....

S.S. FUNNY

ALBERT WHITMAN & Company
Chicago

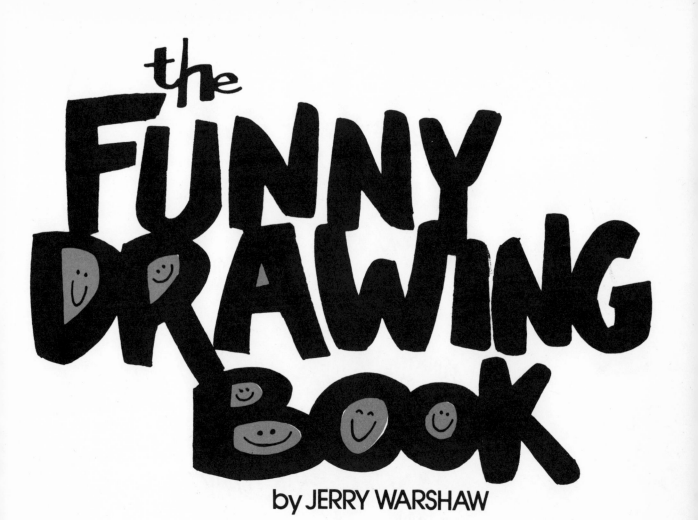

KEEP WATCHING
THE PICTURE PEOPLE...

DRAWING
IS FUN!
FUN
IS DRAWING!
FUNNY DRAWINGS
ARE FUN!
DRAWING FOR FUN
IS FUNNY!
SO
HAVE FUN!

Library of Congress Cataloging in Publication Data
Warshaw, Jerry.
The funny drawing book.
1. Cartooning. I. Masek, Dick. II. Title.
NC1320.W38 741.5 77-14389
ISBN 0-8075-2681-9

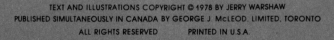

TO CAROLINE RUBIN- FRIEND AND MENTOR- THANKS!

Why a funny drawing book?
Because drawing is fun, and making funny pictures is more fun, and telling funny stories with funny pictures is the MOST fun of all. (Gasp!)

I DIDN'T KNOW CATS COULD TALK!
THEY CAN'T HE'S JUST PRETENDING!

Let's begin, just for fun,
with ARTISTIC SHAPES.

What are artistic shapes?
They're circles and squares
and triangles and lots more
that an artist draws.
Who's the artist? YOU!

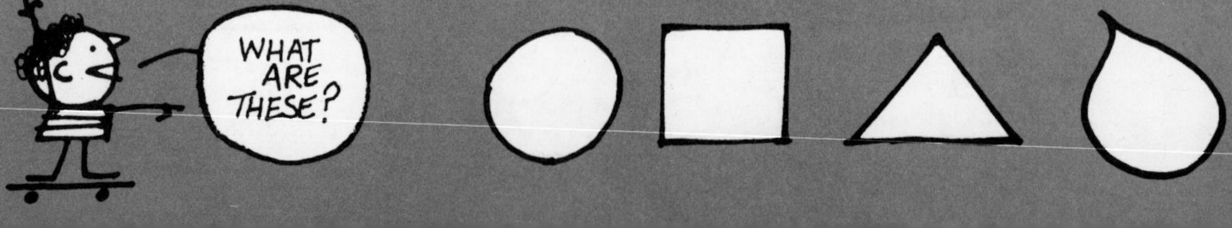

DID HE DO THIS ON PURPOSE?
?
What is it? It's an artistic circle because it's MY circle.
I'm glad you told me— it is your kind of circle.
Now let me draw MY artistic circle.

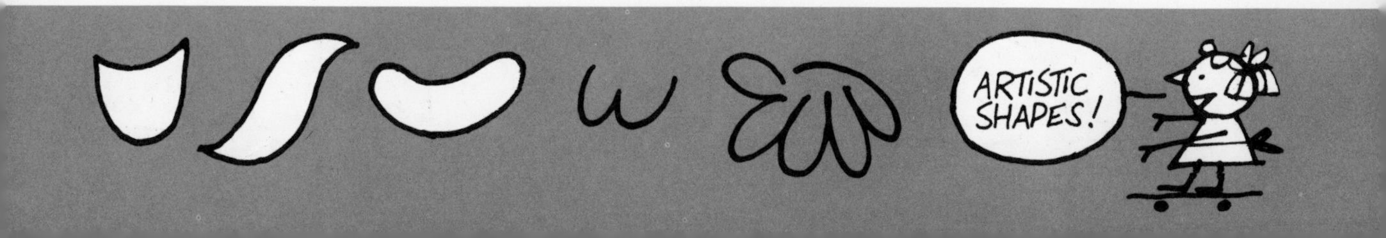
ARTISTIC SHAPES!

Just looking at these ARTISTIC SHAPES can give you ideas. All right—draw the shapes your own way, and you'll really begin to have fun.

Drawing is just putting these shapes together to make pictures.
ARTISTIC CIRCLE
Learn to look.
ARTISTIC TRIANGLE
Notice how many things have the same basic shape.
Keep it simple.
ARTISTIC SQUARE
It's called artistic because it's the way you wanted to draw it.
ARTISTIC RECTANGLE
Unless you say you've made a mistake, others might not know.
ARTISTIC TEARDROP
Take the shape and turn it different ways.
ARTISTIC HOT DOG

ONLY YOU KNOW IF YOU'RE WRONG!
BE YOURSELF — DON'T COPY!
BE YOURSELF— DON'T COPY!

Experiment—
try different kinds of paper
and different drawing materials.
ARTISTIC HOT DOG

Carry a
sketch
pad.
Compose pictures
by looking through
a camera viewfinder.
ARTISTIC RECTANGLE

Use your imagination.
ARTISTIC HALF-MOON

Squint at an object,
then you'll see
the basic shape.
ARTISTIC LEAF

Think of your
drawing as a stage
and you are the director.
ARTISTIC TRIANGLE

DON'T DRAW ON OR IN A BOOK!
DON'T FORGET TO SIGN YOUR DRAWINGS!

Now look around with an artist's eyes—
that means with YOUR eyes.

It's strange, but everywhere you look,
you see ARTISTIC SHAPES.

What's that mean?

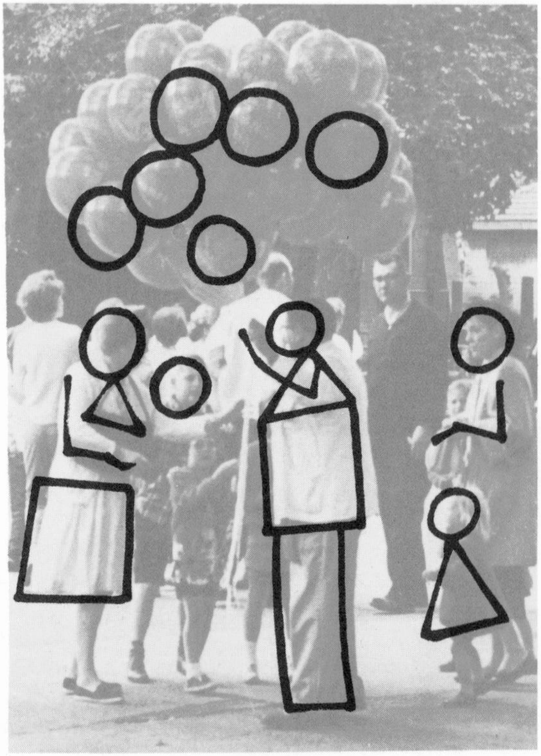

I LIKE THOSE SHAPES!
I LIKE SOME OF THEM!

It means you can draw all these things
and make your own funny pictures.

SAY–IF YOU PUT THOSE SHAPES TOGETHER....
–YOU GET PICTURES!

**There's another way to have fun with artistic shapes.
Take the same shape, add to it, move it around—see what happens.**

Suppose you begin with a hot dog but you want to draw HORSES.

Add a neck and a tail

head and ears

mane and eye,

legs and hoofs—
a horse!

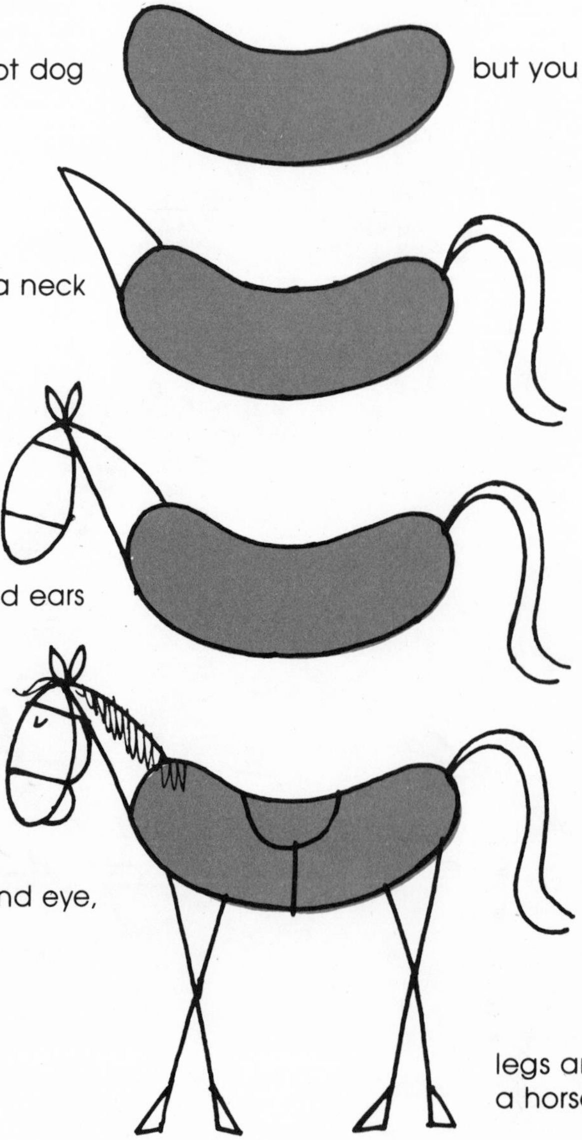

Pretty soon you can have a whole stable of horses, and horse's cousins, too.

Farm horse

Bronco

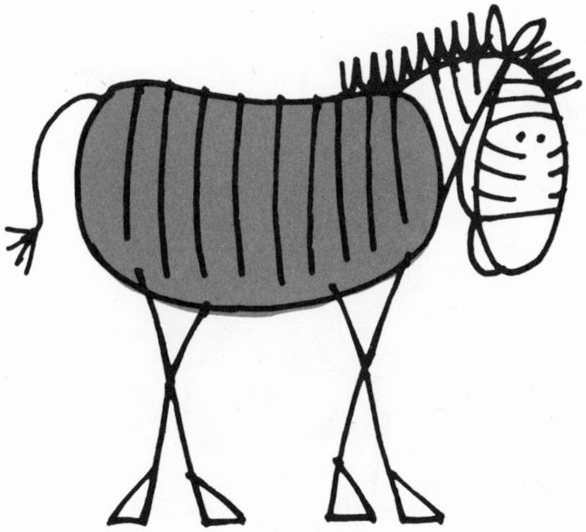

Zebra

Mule—mean isn't he?

HOW DO WE KNOW THEY'RE HOT DOGS?
BECAUSE THEY'VE BEEN OUT IN THE SUN ALL DAY!

Making funny pictures is fun all by itself.

Cats, kittens, big cats, little cats.

People—little, big, middle-sized, old, all kinds.

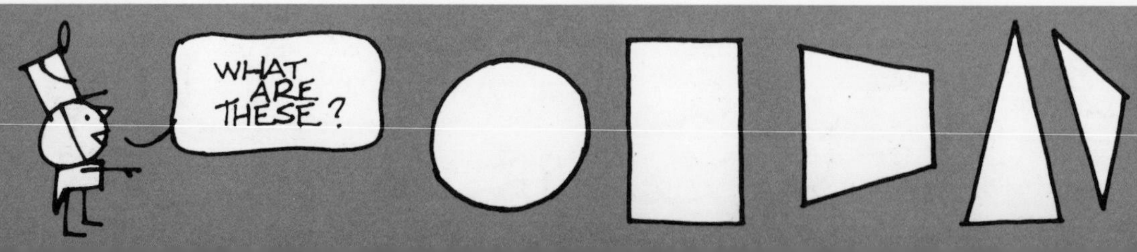

Those cats and people can make you smile, but they're not exactly funny pictures by themselves. How about putting two things together? It can be funny, like a joke, because one thing tells you something about the other.

Now how about this man—is he a midget or a giant? Is that a tree or a bush?

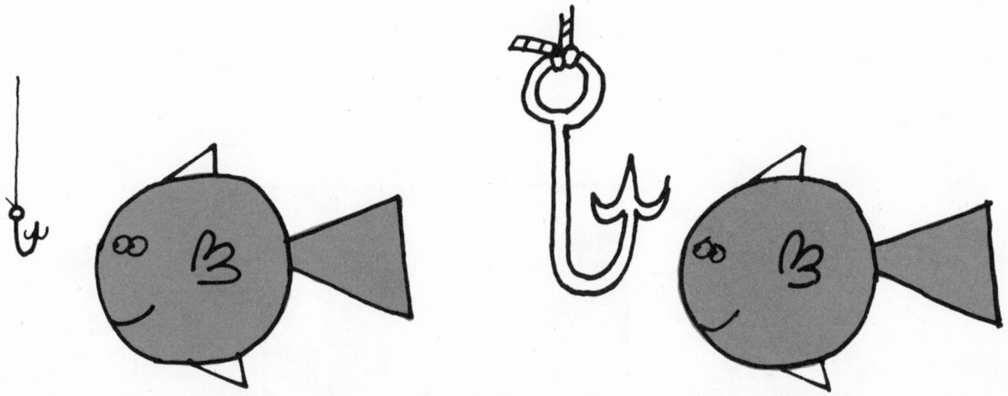

Are there two fish, one big and one little? Or are there two hooks, one little, and one big? You tell me!

Fool your friends with drawings like these. Let them guess, then tell them it's really something quite different.

JUST MORE WAYS TO MAKE THE ARTISTIC SHAPES!

What can you do with your funny pictures, besides laugh at them? You can tell a story aloud as you draw, like this:

Here's a box,
just a plain box.

No, it's a box turtle,
sleepwalking ...

Well, now it's
an elephant.

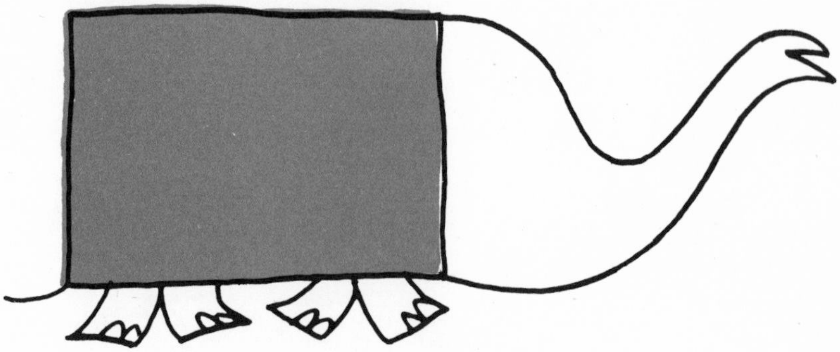

Another elephant? No, no!

A ball bounces along, like this: 

And now I've drawn . . .

Try that funny picture for a start.
Then next time make it your own story with a new twist.

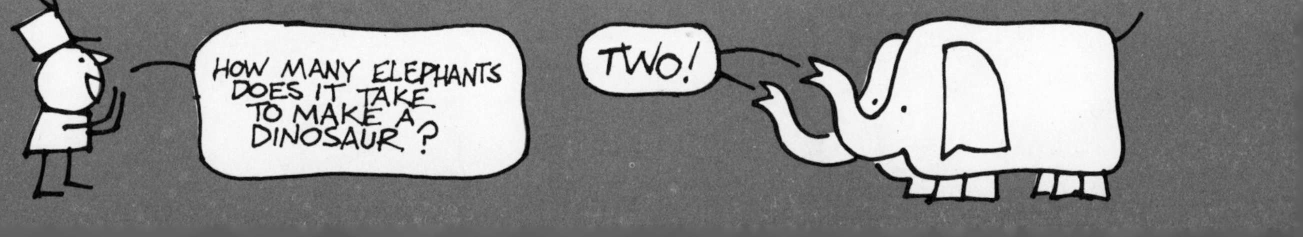

There are two ways to use funny pictures when you tell a story.
First, you can begin with the picture and make the story go with it. That's what we've just been doing.
OR, you can begin with the story AND draw the funny pictures to go with it.
Like this ...

THERE ARE SOME FUNNY IDEAS IN THIS BOOK?

Here's my story about a cat that likes to daydream.

AND SOME FUNNY CATS TOO!

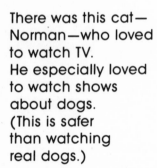

There was this cat—
Norman—who loved
to watch TV.
He especially loved
to watch shows
about dogs.
(This is safer
than watching
real dogs.)

But Norman didn't
like the commercials.
They were usually
about dog food.
Yeccch!
So during the
commercials, he
would turn around
and daydream—
that he was a LION!

His pointed ears
would become
round ...

ALL DOMESTIC CATS HAVE POINTED EARS!
MOST WILD CATS HAVE ROUND EARS!

And his nose
would grow longer,
and he'd get a
mean look.
(Or maybe it
was only a
nearsighted look.)

And he dreamed
that he lived
in a really
exclusive zoo,
where his mane
was brushed and
combed every day,
and he felt good
and well groomed.

But then one day,
he was sent to
another zoo—
not as fine
and as exclusive
as the first one.

REMEMBER!
KEEP IT SIMPLE!

The zoo director
was so stingy that
there weren't keepers
to comb and brush
the lions.
So Norman's mane
got all tacky.

And the director was
also very stingy
about spending
money on repairs.
So holes appeared
in the roof—and when
it rained,
WOW!

And as if that
wasn't enough
to think about,
Norman thought
he saw …

SEE WHAT A GENTLE LION NORMAN IS!

a CROCODILE!

But he woke up
just in time
and …

He went back
to watching TV,
feeling that,
after all,
dogs are easier
to deal with
than crocodiles.

I SEE—BUT
I'M SURE GLAD
HE WOKE UP
IN TIME!

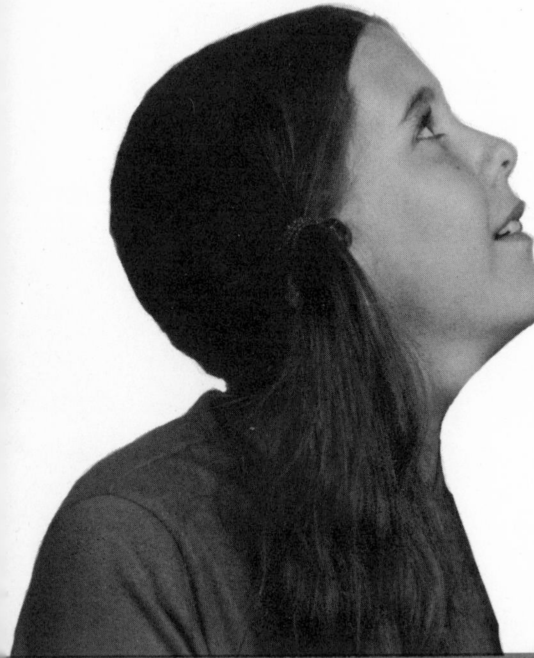

Look around for ideas— even up in the sky.

If you have trouble getting ideas— just for the fun of it—look at some clouds and see what you can imagine in them. Even when you look at clouds you can also see those artistic shapes. That helps you start your own drawing.

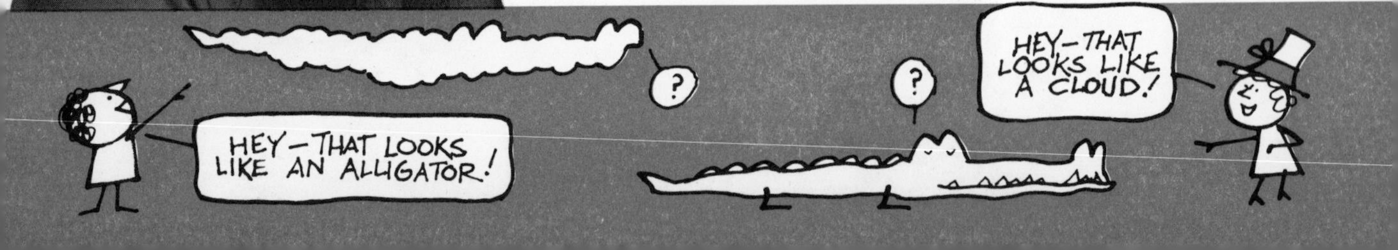

HEY—THAT LOOKS LIKE AN ALLIGATOR!
?
?
HEY—THAT LOOKS LIKE A CLOUD!

Suppose you look at these photographs.
Do you see the same artistic shapes that
I saw? Maybe you see different ones.
That's OK. Artists don't have to agree.
Find photographs in a magazine or newspaper
and try an artistic shapes hide-and-seek
game. See how many shapes you can trace.

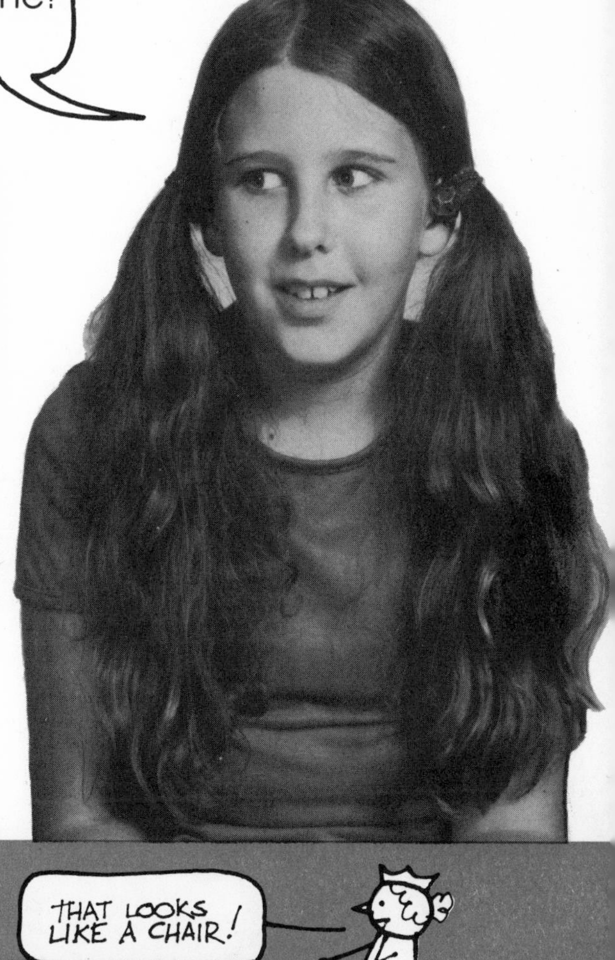

I saw a face in the phone!

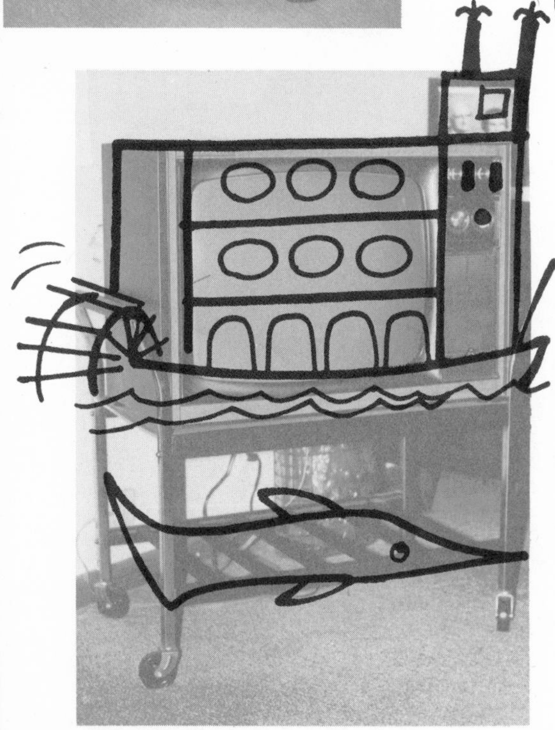

THAT LOOKS LIKE A FROG!
THAT LOOKS LIKE A CHAIR!

Sometimes when you put two very different ideas together you have the beginning of a story.

Here are some STORY STARTERS:

A lion and an owl

A school crossing guard and an elephant

WHY DOES HE DRAW SO MANY ANIMALS?
BECAUSE ANIMALS DON'T TELL YOU HOW TO DRAW!

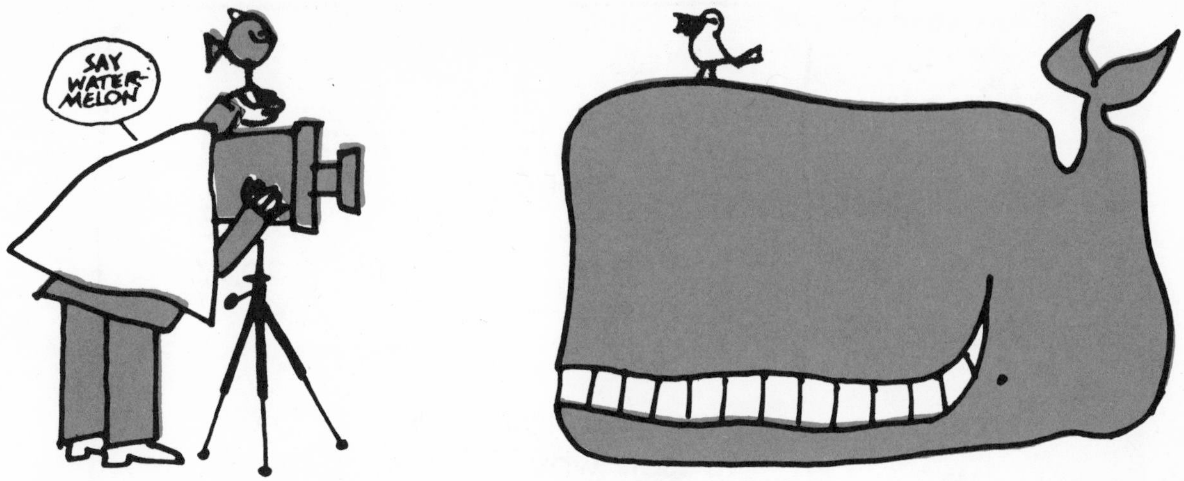

A man with a camera—and a whale

Thinking about how people feel is another way to get started. Here's more about feelings and drawing expressions.

Make up a story about something that happened—then show how three different people would react to the same thing happening.

Here's how three people felt when someone said,
"The boiler broke down, so school will close early today."

You | Your teacher (who really likes kids) | Your mom

When you draw an expression on someone's face (happy, sad, mad, surprised—whatever), you have to know how happy, sad, mad, or surprised the person is.

And you have to know the reason why the person feels that way.

KEEP IT SIMPLE!

Here's a story about a girl who had an interesting day. You'll see why ...

IT'S SIMPLY INTERESTING!

1

One morning, this girl—we'll call her Elizabeth—woke up, looked at the alarm clock, and said, "Oh, gosh! It's nine o'clock. I'll be late for school."

2

Then she remembered it was Saturday and there was no school. And she didn't have any homework to do, either.

5

Who cares about hats? There'll be a big birthday cake with candles, and all her friends are coming.

6

And they'll bring presents
and sing
HAPPY BIRTHDAY!
and everything.

3

AND it was her birthday!
I forget which one—eight or nine?
Or maybe ten. Oh, yes, ten!

4

She was going to have a party with funny hats and favors and games. But wait! Nobody got the hats. How can you have a birthday party without silly hats?

7

Then her grandfather is coming from California and bringing a big two-wheeler bicycle with all the junk on it ...

8

And after the party, her whole family will get on an airplane and fly to Hawaii!

IF YOU ARE ALREADY IN HAWAII— PICK ANOTHER CITY!
EAST WARD!

Need a model?

Now that we've told you what can happen to Elizabeth on an interesting day, let's see what can happen to you.

Take a large piece of paper and something to draw with. Then sit down before a mirror and begin to tell yourself stories.

HEY - I'VE GOT A STORY FOR YOU!
I CAN SEE IT IN YOUR FACE!

See what happens to your face.

I found a magic penny.

A giant dragon was chasing me!

My brother broke my favorite doll.

SHE'S MAKING FACES—
—WHILE SHE'S MAKING FACES!

Everybody likes pictures and stories about people.

People walking ...

People standing ...

When you draw people doing things, begin with the ARTISTIC SHAPES and draw people as you see them.

... or maybe running?

How do they feel?

Let's see what people do and how you tell what they're feeling.

People sitting ...

People doing all kinds of funny things ...

Here are more people doing more things. Do they give you ideas?

... on all kinds of chairs.

Look at those expressions!

Now, how about some backgrounds for the people you draw? Start with the ARTISTIC SHAPES. Soon the people and backgrounds will fit together to make a FUNNY PICTURE.

Some apartment buildings have windows like this.
Or this.
Or this.

SAY–THEY'RE ALL MADE OUT OF THE ARTISTIC SHAPES!
RIGHT! NOW YOU'VE GOT IT!

Ideas? Look around for them.

All right— trees can give you ideas.

Something lives in here.

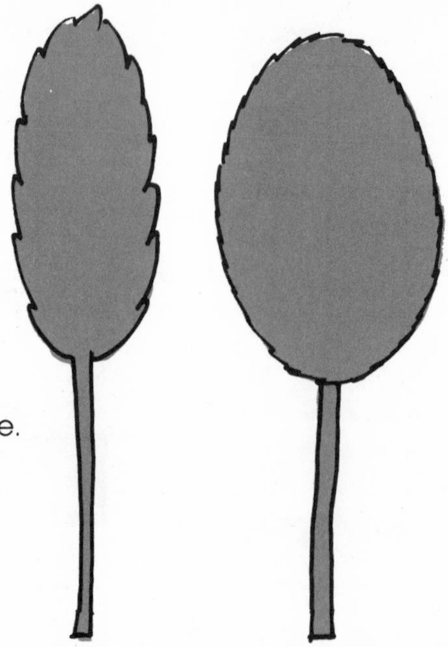

Some trees look like lollipops.

Some have to be protectec

Some trees look great in winter.

Here's a busy-looking tree.

Bushes or trees?

I LIKE TREES!
WATCH OUT FOR THE COCONUTS!
REMEMBER—A TREE IS ALWAYS REACHING FOR THE SUN!
THAT'S WHY THE BRANCHES GO UP!

Ready to draw a funny picture that tells a story all by itself?

"A Day in the Life of a Crossing Guard"

Before you start, you have to ask yourself some questions.

Is the crossing guard a man or a woman?
How old are the children?
Are they on their way home?
Is it a busy street?
Is she young or old? Fat or thin?
Are they going to school?
How many kids are there?
Is this a big city or a small town?

Let's commence PICTURE BUILDING.

First we draw the street and the crossing guard.

Now, how can we make this a funny picture?

SAY—I STILL HAVE SOME MORE QUESTIONS!
GREAT! GET ALL THE INFORMATION YOU CAN!

It's time to add to the picture you're building.

We draw the children ...

AND REMEMBER!
REMEMBER WHAT?

And now see what happens!

and then we draw the background and add the details.

Look! Something funny walked right into the picture!
And that's how to draw a funny picture. Now start your own.

Now try a comic strip of your own.

It's a good idea to get to know your main characters. What they do tells a lot about how they feel.

Begin with a page of character sketches. Just for fun, let's say the main characters are a little boy and his dog.
See how you get to know them?
And you don't even need any words.

BUSY-AREN'T THEY?
BUT I FEEL I KNOW THEM!

A COMIC STRIP calls for special PICTURE BUILDING.

Now that we have our main characters, let's try a comic strip.

What are we trying to do?
To tell a joke in pictures!

Here's the same joke told two ways, with the same characters. First, all panels are drawn as you'd see them from one angle.

Here we tell where the action is.

Here we set up the joke.

The "straight" line— it gets ready for the joke.

The joke.

WHAT SHOULD WE REMEMBER?

Here's the same joke, but the action is seen from different angles. This way, the action is more like what you see in a movie.

Besides just a joke-a-day strip, you can do a continued story. The story takes several strips to tell, but each strip ends with a joke.

We hope you've had fun drawing with us and will go on having a happy drawing time.

I DIDN'T KNOW CATS COULD DRAW!
OH SURE— BUT JUST FOR FUN!